To Mr Toad

Ladybird books are widely available, but in case of difficulty may be ordered by post or telephone from:

Ladybird Books – Cash Sales Department Littlegate Road Paignton Devon TQ3 3BE
Telephone 01803 554761

A catalogue record for this book is available from the British Library

Published by Ladybird Books Ltd Loughborough Leicestershire UK
Ladybird Books Ltd is a subsidiary of the Penguin Group of companies
© Colin and Valerie King MCMXCVI
The author/artist have asserted their moral rights
LADYBIRD and the device of a Ladybird are trademarks of Ladybird Books Ltd

In comes the tide

Colin and Valerie King

Picture
Ladybird

In comes the tide, over slimy green rocks.

Out goes the tide, washing everyone's socks.

 In comes the tide, bringing billowing sails.

Out goes the tide, taking sea-spouting whales.

In comes the tide, splashing pirates of old.

Out goes the tide, leaving cargoes of gold.

 In comes the tide, with sea horses prancing.

Out goes the tide, crusty lobsters are dancing.

In comes the tide, bringing Neptune the King.

Out goes the tide, leaving jellies that sting.

 In comes the tide, with gigantic white waves.

Out goes the tide, over shipwrecks and caves.

 In comes the tide, on a bright, moonlit night.

Out goes the tide, it's a smuggler's delight.

 In comes the tide, see the octopus wobbling.

Out goes the tide, leaving walruses squabbling.

 In comes the tide, the Admiral has landed.

Out goes the tide, all his shipmates are stranded.

 In comes the tide, to islands of sun.

Out goes the tide, while monkeys have fun.

 In comes the tide, bringing fishermen home.

Out goes the tide, rolling seals in the foam.

 In comes the tide, with a thunderous roar.

Out goes the tide, to some other shore.

Picture Ladybird

Books for reading aloud with 2–6 year olds

The exciting *Picture Ladybird* series includes a wide range
of animal stories, funny rhymes, and real life adventures that are
perfect to read aloud and share at storytime or bedtime.

A whole library of beautiful books for you to collect

RHYMING STORIES

Easy to follow and great for joining in!

Jasper's Jungle Journey, Val Biro
Shoo Fly, Shoo! Brian Moses
Ten Tall Giraffes, Brian Moses
In Comes the Tide, Valerie King
Toot! Learns to Fly,
Geraldine Taylor & Jill Harker
Who Am I? Judith Nicholls
Fly Eagle, Fly! Jan Pollard

IMAGINATIVE TALES

Mysterious and magical, or just a little shivery

The Star that Fell, Karen Hayles
Wishing Moon, Lesley Harker
Don't Worry William, Christine Morton
This Way Little Badger, Phil McMylor
The Giant Walks, Judith Nicholls
Kelly and the Mermaid, Karen King

FUNNY STORIES

Make storytime good fun!

Benedict Goes to the Beach, Chris Demarest
Bella and Gertie, Geraldine Taylor
Edward Goes Exploring, David Pace
Telephone Ted, Joan Stimson
Top Shelf Ted, Joan Stimson
Helpful Henry, Shen Roddie
What's Wrong with Bertie? Tony Bradman
Bears Can't Fly, Val Biro
Finnigan's Flap, Joan Stimson

REAL LIFE ADVENTURE

Situations to explore and discover

Joe and the Farm Goose,
Geraldine Taylor & Jill Harker
Going to Playgroup,
Geraldine Taylor & Jill Harker
The Great Rabbit Race, Geraldine Taylor
Pushchair Polly, Tony Bradman

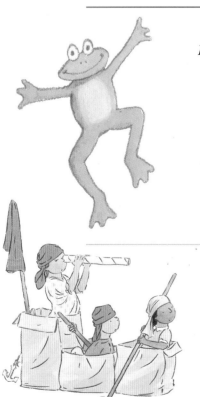